AUSSIE BITES

Goldfever

It's Grand Final day, and Austin is
the champion full-forward of his team.
Just before the game, he discovers
a gold nugget, right in the middle of
the footy field. But he doesn't want
anyone to find out.

which Aussie Bites have **you** read?

 yes **GOLDFEVER**
Justin D'Ath
Illustrated by Rachel Tonkin

 MOVING HOUSE
James Moloney
Illustrated by Tom Jellett

 S.N.A.G.
Margaret Clark
Illustrated by Terry Denton

 BATTER UP!
Sherryl Clark
Illustrated by Chantal Stewart

 MISS WOLF AND THE PORKERS
Bill Condon
Illustrated by Caroline Magerl

 JALEESA THE EMU
Nola Kerr and Susannah Brindle
Illustrated by Craig Charles

Aussie Bites

Goldfever

Justin D'Ath

Illustrated by Rachel Tonkin

Puffin Books

For the Holton boys. *J.D.*
For Patrick. *R.T.*

Puffin Books
Penguin Books Australia Ltd
487 Maroondah Highway, PO Box 257
Ringwood, Victoria 3134, Australia
Penguin Books Ltd
Harmondsworth, Middlesex, England
Penguin Putnam Inc.
375 Hudson Street, New York, New York 10014, USA
Penguin Books Canada Limited
10 Alcorn Avenue, Toronto, Ontario, Canada, M4V 3B2
Penguin Books (N.Z.) Ltd
Cnr Rosedale and Airborne Roads, Albany, Auckland, New Zealand
Penguin Books (South Africa) (Pty) Ltd
5 Watkins Street, Denver Ext 4, 2094, South Africa
Penguin Books India (P) Ltd
11, Community Centre, Panchsheel Park, New Delhi 110 017, India

First published by Penguin Books Australia, 2001

1 3 5 7 9 10 8 6 4 2

Text copyright © Justin D'Ath, 2001
Illustrations copyright © Rachel Tonkin, 2001

The moral right of the author and illustrator has been asserted.

Designed by Melissa Fraser, Penguin Design Studio
Series designed by Ruth Grüner
Series editor: Kay Ronai
Typeset in New Century School Book
by Post Pre-press Group, Brisbane, Queensland
Made and printed in Australia by Australian Print Group,
Maryborough, Victoria

National Library of Australia
Cataloguing-in-Publication data:
D'Ath, Justin.
Goldfever.
ISBN 0 14 130939 3.
I. Tonkin, Rachel. II. Title. (Series: Aussie bites).
A823.3

www.puffin.com.au

1
Grand Final Day

'Austin!'

Someone was shaking my shoulder.

'Austin, time to get up!'

I blinked a couple of times, had a big stretch and a yawn, then glanced sleepily at my bedside clock.

Eight-fifteen! I'd slept in!

Then I remembered.

'Aw, Mum! It's Saturday!'

'Grand Final Day,' she reminded me.

As if I'd forget. 'It doesn't start till
ten-thirty.'

Mum handed me a dog-lead. With
a dog on the end of it. 'So there's
plenty of time to take Bootsie for
a walk before you go.'

Bootsie leapt up onto the bed and gave me a big, drooly slurp in the face. Yuck! I pulled my pillow over my head. 'Can't he have a sleep-in too?'

'He needs a walk,' said Mum. 'He's been cooped up inside for four days now.'

That was when I remembered the rain. It had started on Tuesday and hadn't stopped since.

Or had it?

Lifting one corner of the pillow, I listened carefully. Not a sound.

'Has the rain gone?'

'It stopped at about midnight,' Mum said.

'Excellent!' I sat up, spilling Bootsie off the bed. 'Now I won't have to play in the ruck!'

Normally I was our team's full-forward, but when it rained Mr Barnes, our coach, put me in the

ruck. He reckoned I couldn't kick straight when the ball was wet. All because I had missed three sitters one rainy day early in the season. Luckily there had only been two other wet Saturdays since then, so I had mostly played at full-forward. And I had done pretty well. I had kicked ninety-seven goals – just two short of the Diggers Gully record, set eleven years earlier by Kenny 'Boots' Cooper, when he used to go to our school.

Now he was a champion AFL player and my absolute, number one hero. I'd even named my dog after him.

'Well?' Mum was standing next to my bed, hands on her hips. 'Don't just sit there – Bootsie is waiting.'

But Bootsie wasn't waiting. He was already halfway out my bedroom door, dragging his lead behind him.

2
Legend!

I decided to take Bootsie to Goldmine
Park to check out the condition of the
footy oval.

Even though the rain had stopped,
I was worried the ground might
be boggy. A boggy ground meant
a slippery ball. And a slippery ball
meant Mr Barnes wouldn't let me
play at full-forward.

I was desperate to equal Boots
Cooper's record, maybe even break it.

'Imagine breaking Boots Cooper's record,' I said out loud. 'I'd be a legend!'

Bootsie wagged his tail happily and strained at the end of his lead.

Goldmine Park was right across town. It took us ages to get there. But I wasn't worried – the game didn't start for two more hours. There was heaps of time.

Bootsie and I weren't the only ones at the oval. Two women in tracksuits were power-walking around the boundary; a man was setting up a hot-dog caravan in the car-park; and some boys were kicking goals down at

the creek end. I didn't take much
notice of any of them. Slipping Bootsie
off his leash, I made my way out to
the centre of the ground.

Goldmine Park was new. A year ago
it had been nothing but a patch of
ugly scrubland with a big, weedy

mullock heap in the middle. The mullock heap was from the old goldmine that used to be there. Last summer the council had bulldozed it flat, planted grass and – bingo! – our town had a brand new footy oval.

The ground didn't look too bad. It was damp but there weren't any puddles. The grass was nice and thick, except in the centre-square where it was mostly worn away from all the hit-outs. I walked into the bare patch and tested it with the toe of my right sneaker. It wasn't boggy at all. The yellow clay felt nice and firm.

Maybe I would get to play full-forward after all.

3
Tug-of-war

Bootsie came lolloping up and started jumping all over me.

'You want a game do you, boy?'

I held out his lead. Bootsie clamped his jaws onto the end of it and began pulling. I pulled the other way. Tug-of-war. It was one of our favourite games. Usually I won, but today my foot slipped and I fell flat on my bum. Bootsie bounced away with the lead, flapping it triumphantly in the air.

'You win!' I laughed, scrambling to my feet.

As I wiped the clay and dirt off the back of my jeans, I noticed what had caused me to slip over. A golden chocolate wrapper lay embedded in the yellow clay at my feet.

'Lousy litter-bugs!' I muttered,
bending to pick it up.

Crunch! It nearly broke my
fingernails!

Hey, what was going on?

I had a closer look. The wrapper
was sort of oval-shaped, perfectly flat

and nearly as big as my hand. It *looked* like a chocolate wrapper, but it certainly didn't feel like one. When I ran my fingers over its golden surface, it felt rough. Like a rock.

A golden rock.

Suddenly my mind clicked.

Goldmine Park, golden rock . . .

Gold!

4
Gold in Goldmine Park!

I didn't believe it. No way! People didn't find gold in the middle of footy ovals! It was a practical joke – someone had buried a rock there and painted it.

Gold in Goldmine Park, ha ha ha!

I tried scratching its golden surface with my thumbnail. The gold wouldn't come off.

So it wasn't paint.

'It *does* look like gold,' I said

16

to Bootsie. 'And there *did* used to be

a goldmine here . . .'

BOUNCE!

A football landed two metres away

and whizzed off over my head.

Startled, I looked around. One of

the boys from down near the goals

was running towards me. Uh-oh!

Quickly I straightened up.

And stood on the rock.

'Sorry,' puffed the boy, trotting up

to Bootsie, who had fetched the ball

and was hoping for a game of tug-of-

war with it. 'That one went a bit long.'

'Drop it, Bootsie!' I said.

The boy picked up the ball and wiped it on his sleeve. He was about my age and quite tall. I knew him from somewhere.

'Lost something?' he asked me, looking curiously at my feet.

I felt my face go red. My sneakers were right together, like the feet of a soldier standing at attention. 'No,' I stammered. 'I was . . . just doing up my laces.'

'You're the full-forward from Diggers Gully, aren't you?'

Now I recognised him – his name was Ryan and he played for Red Hills,

the other team in the Grand Final.
I nodded. 'It's good that the rain's
stopped.'

'Sure is.' Ryan bounced the ball.
'We're having a few kicks. Want to join
us?'

'No thanks. I'm walking my dog.'

He nodded. 'Catch you later then.'

I watched Ryan lope off down
the oval towards his friends, bouncing
the ball ahead of him.

'That was a close call,' I said to
Bootsie, stepping off the golden rock.
'Let's dig this up and get out of here!'

5
Red Sitter

It wouldn't budge. The rock was embedded firmly in the clay.

I stood up and scratched my head. What was I going to do?

I needed to get something to dig it up with. But if I left the rock unguarded, Ryan or one of his friends might find it.

I had an idea.

'Bootsie,' I called. 'Come here.'

He trotted over, wagging his tail.

'Sit!' I commanded.

Right on the golden rock.

Bootsie wasn't exactly the world's best-trained dog, but one thing he could do well was sit. The lady we bought him from said he was a Red Setter, but I reckon he was a new sort of dog – a Red Sitter!

Leaving him on guard duty, I hurried towards the car-park, hoping to find something to dig the rock up with.

'What's the matter with your dog?' the man at the hot-dog caravan asked as I went past.

'Nothing. I'm training him.'

Near the car-park entrance there was a row of iron fence pickets. I found a wobbly one and yanked it out of the ground. It had a nice pointed end, exactly what I needed.

On the way back, I passed the hot-dog man again. He was frowning in the direction of Bootsie, sitting all alone in the middle of the oval.

'What are you training him to do?'

'Meditation,' I said, ducking back under the fence.

Bootsie was pleased to see me come back. I told him to move and he jumped up off the rock. While I was away, the sun had broken through the clouds. It shone on the rock, making it sparkle like . . . well, like gold.

I was certain now that it *was* gold. A humungous gold nugget!

It must have been there all season. I imagined it lying there, just below the surface, while hundreds of footy players (including me) had trampled

backwards and forwards over it.
None of us realised there was gold
just below our feet!

All the rain we'd had over the last
four days had finally uncovered it.

I had no idea how big the nugget
was. All I could see was the top of it,

and that was nearly the size of my hand. The part of it that was still buried might have been HUGE.

'We could be millionaires!' I said to Bootsie.

6
Kung-fu

Aiming its pointed end at the edge of
the nugget, I lifted the fence picket
above my head like a harpoon.

'HEY!' shouted a woman's voice.
The power-walkers had stopped going
round the boundary and were glaring
in my direction. 'WHAT DO YOU
THINK YOU'RE DOING?'

I froze. The hot-dog man and Ryan
and his friends were watching me, too.

'I'm . . . um . . . practising kung-fu!'

Instead of plunging it into the ground, I twirled the picket above my head like a fighting stick, then gripped its ends in both hands and kicked out behind me with my left foot. Next, I did a one-legged jump and twisted my body around in a 180 degree spin.

Out of the corner of my eye,
I looked to see if anyone was still
watching me. The two women had got
back to their power-walking, but the
hot-dog man still seemed interested.
Ryan and his friends were shaking
their heads and laughing among
themselves.

I felt like a complete bozo!

I did a few more kung-fu moves,
then bent forward, pretending I was
doing a stretching exercise. Really I
was looking at the giant gold nugget.
And trying to work out what to do.

7
Finders Keepers

It was a big problem. If I dug up the nugget while everyone was watching, they would probably try to take it away from me. I wasn't sure what the law said about finding gold on a public oval, but most likely the town council would say it belonged to them.

It wasn't fair! I had found it, I should be allowed to keep it. Finders keepers!

Suddenly I knew what I had to do.

I would come back that night and dig the nugget up in the dark. That way nobody would see me.

The only problem with that plan was the Grand Final. In a couple of hours there would be thirty-six blokes charging backwards and forwards over this spot. Someone was bound to notice it. Unless . . .

I looked up at the sky. It was still pretty cloudy.

Rain, I thought. Please rain!

8
Distant Thunder

It didn't rain.

'Right.' Mr Barnes consulted his team-plan. 'Austin, you're full-forward.'

'Can't I be ruckman?'

If I were ruckman, I could be near the nugget. I could even stand on it, if I had to. Anything to keep the other players away from it.

'Did I hear you correctly?' asked Mr Barnes.

Everyone was looking at me in amazement. They knew how close I was to breaking Boots Cooper's record.

'The grass *is* pretty wet . . .' I said lamely.

The coach put an arm around my shoulder. 'I know you're nervous,

34

Austin. We all are. This is the big one.
We need your fire-power up forward.'

I couldn't get out of it. And Mr
Barnes was right – the team needed
me.

But I wasn't thinking about the
team, I was thinking about the gold.
I had a bad case of goldfever!

On my way to the forward line,
I made a casual detour through the
centre-square.

I nearly trod on the nugget before
I saw it.

Excellent! The camouflage was
working. Before I took Bootsie home,
I had smeared the nugget's golden

surface with mud so it wouldn't look so obvious.

It was nearly invisible.

As I trotted down to the goal square, I had my fingers crossed. Maybe things would work out all right, after all.

There was a distant rumble of thunder.

9
Ninety-nine

The first quarter went well for Diggers Gully. When the siren went we were four goals up on Red Hills. Two of those goals were kicked by yours truly.

Ninety-nine. I had equalled Boots Cooper's record.

One more goal and I'd be a legend!

Mr Barnes clapped me on the back at quarter-time. 'Keep it up, Austin!'

But I didn't keep it up. I couldn't.

Because the ball didn't come past our half-forward line once in the entire second quarter. It kept going the other way.

All I could do was stand and watch as Red Hills kicked eight goals down the other end of the ground.

We were all feeling pretty dejected as we trudged over to the boundary line at half-time.

10
Team Game

'I've got a surprise for you,' Mr Barnes told us as we gathered round him for his half-time address. 'Because today is such a special occasion, I've brought along an assistant coach.'

We groaned. The last thing we needed was *two* coaches to tell us what we'd been doing wrong!

Mr Barnes stood aside to let someone through. 'I'm sure you all know this bloke,' he said.

My jaw dropped. In fact, about twenty jaws dropped.

It was Kenny Boots Cooper!

'Sorry I'm late, fellas,' he said with a smile. 'Thought I'd drop in to see my old team win the flag.'

I couldn't believe it. It really was him!

'We, um, aren't exactly winning,' someone said.

Boots Cooper grinned. He was nearly as tall as a goal post. 'It's only

half-time. The game is still there to be won.'

'He's right.' Mr Barnes stepped forward. 'Kenny and I have been talking, and we have decided to make a few position changes. Austin, we want you to go into the ruck . . . '

'*What?*' I gasped. In the excitement of the game, I had nearly forgotten the gold nugget. It was safe under its camouflage. 'But I only need one more goal!'

Mr Barnes sounded apologetic. 'You're not going to kick any more goals if the ball keeps going the other way.'

I wasn't going to kick any goals
from the centre-square, either.
Mr Barnes didn't like the ruckman
going forward, except to contest
bounces and throw-ins.

Boots Cooper put one giant hand
on my shoulder. I didn't hear what he

said because at the exact moment that he opened his mouth there was a loud rumble of thunder.

'Pardon?'

'It's a team game, Austin. What's important are the goals, not who scores them.'

11
Doh!

The Red Hills ruckman grinned at me across the centre-circle.

'Well, look who it is – Mr Kung-fu himself!'

'Gidday, Ryan,' I said.

I was watching the umpire. He was about to bounce the ball.

Right on top of the gold nugget!

Even from ten metres away, I could see it as plain as day. The dirt I'd smeared on it earlier had all worn off!

Whap! The ball hit one corner
of the nugget and zinged away like
a rocket. Ryan was already racing in
for the hit-out, but I wasn't moving.

I stood rooted to the spot.

I wasn't watching the ball, I was
watching the umpire. He was

47

frowning down at the ground. Directly at the nugget!

I was sunk. Mr Barnes wasn't letting me break Boots Cooper's record, and now I was going to lose the gold!

Something hit me on the chest.

My hands clasped it automatically.
It was the ball. The crooked bounce
had come straight to me!

Suddenly I was angry. *Team game!*
I scoffed. *Boots Cooper probably didn't*
want *me to break his record!*

Ryan was charging at me like a
steam train. I turned and ran. Right
out of the centre-square. *Who cared*
about Mr Barnes and his silly rules!
Straight down the ground. Players
were coming at me from all directions.
My team-mates were calling for the
ball; about ten Red Hills players were
closing in. I sidestepped nimbly
around someone, weaved my way

between three more. All I was focused
on were the goals. The crowd was
going mental, screaming and shouting
and cheering. It was awesome!

Suddenly a hand came out of

nowhere and latched onto my arm.
It was Ryan. No way, I said to myself.
No way was anybody going to stop me
now! I spun out of his tackle and
raced away from him. Eat my dust,
Ryan!

The goals were just ahead. I lined
them up. Dropping the ball onto my
boot, I sent it spiralling straight
between the uprights. Yesssssss!

One hundred!

There goes your record, Boots
Cooper!

Instead of signalling a goal,
the goal-umpire stood there like
a stunned mullet.

'Good one, Kung-fu!' Ryan clapped me on the back. 'You just scored a goal for us!'

Doh! I was at the wrong end of the ground!

12
Guarding the Nugget

Luckily the goal didn't count. In Aussie Rules you can't score a goal for the other team. It wasn't even a point because I had run too far without bouncing the ball.

Red Hills got a free kick just on their side of the centre-square.

I felt like a real fruit loop. Imagine doing that in front of all those people! In front of Boots Cooper!

But one good thing came out of it.

The umpire had been so surprised to see a player running the wrong way that he seemed to have forgotten all about the gold nugget.

As soon as Ryan had taken the free kick, and everyone's attention was down on the Red Hills half-forward line, I wandered back to the centre-square and innocently cleaned the mud off the bottom of my boots. And trampled it all over the gold nugget.

By the time I was finished, the nugget was nearly invisible again.

I spent the rest of the quarter being a ruckman. And guarding the nugget. Whenever the ball came within ten metres of it – or when there was a bounce – I thumped it down towards our goals as hard as I could. I think I must have won every hit-out.

By three-quarter time Diggers Gully was only two goals behind.

13
It Looks Like Rain

Mr Barnes went right off at me.

'What the dickens did you think you were doing? If you want to kick goals for Red Hills, you'd better change schools!'

I hung my head. Maybe I *would* change schools. With all the money I was going to get for the gold nugget, Mum and I could go and live on the Gold Coast.

'Don't be too hard on him, coach,'

Boots Cooper said. 'He's the reason we've closed the gap to just two goals.'

I caught Mr Barnes's eye. 'Can I go back onto the forward line this quarter?'

He shook his head. 'You're too valuable where you are. Besides' – he pointed at the sky – 'it looks like it might rain.'

There was a long, low rumble of thunder.

14
Screamer!

The storm hit late in the final quarter.

For twenty minutes the thunder
had been growing louder and louder.
A wind sprang up. It was gentle at
first, but gradually it grew stronger.
Semi-darkness fell across the oval as
a towering bank of blue–black clouds
rolled ominously overhead.

Lightning flashed and flickered
in the clouds. Thunder shook the air.

It started to rain.

'Stop the game!' someone yelled from the boundary line. 'Someone might get struck by lightning!'

The umpire was about to bounce the ball after another goal by our team. Diggers Gully was only two points behind! He looked at his watch.

'Keep playing!' shouted Mr Barnes.

Everyone in our team agreed with him. If the umpire stopped the game now, we would lose!

'Two more minutes,' the umpire said.

He bounced the ball.

This time I was caught flat-footed. Ryan got to the ball first and punched it over my head. A Red Hills player grabbed it out of the air and speared it into their half-forward line. Two kicks later, their full-forward took a mark on his chest. He was only twenty metres out from the goal and directly in front. I groaned.

'Looks like you guys are dead and
buried,' Ryan sniggered.

I kept my mouth shut. Ryan and
I stood side-by-side in the centre-
square, watching his team's full-
forward line up the goals. My fingers
were crossed. It wasn't such an easy

kick, straight into the wind and the
rain.

There was a huge crash of thunder
just as the full-forward took his kick.
The ball slewed sideways off his boot.
It was only a behind.

'Not quite dead and buried,' I
muttered.

Ryan bumped me with his shoulder. 'As if you could win now, Kung-fu!' he jeered.

Our full-back kicked the ball in. There was a scramble of players where it landed. I lost sight of the ball. The umpire blew his whistle. Free kick!

One of my team had the ball. I tried to see who it was. Kevin Albury, our half-back. He wasn't a very long kick of the footy. I started to move forwards. Ryan came with me.

The ball sailed through the air. Kevin had unloaded with a mighty torp. The wind caught the ball –

it was going to go clean over our heads! I changed directions, ran back with the flight of the ball. Ryan was hot on my heels; I could hear him just behind me. But I kept my eyes on the ball. At the last moment, I launched myself upwards.

Thump! Ryan's elbow crunched me in the back of the head. I lost sight of the ball. Then I was falling. I landed flat on my face in the wet clay.

The umpire's whistle blew.

There, in my outstretched hands, was the ball.

I had taken a screamer!

15
Kick it High!

The final siren blew just as I was picking myself up off the ground.

A cheer went up from all the Red Hills players and from their supporters in the crowd. They thought they had won.

'Hang on!' I yelled. 'I took a mark!'

Ryan laughed. 'As if you could kick a goal from here!'

He had a point. I was in the centre-circle. It was sixty-five metres to the goal.

'Let him take his kick!' a man's voice was yelling.

I looked over and saw Boots Cooper on the boundary line. He caught my eye and made an upwards motion with his arms.

'Kick it high, Austin!'

Suddenly I realised what he was getting at. The wind. It was blowing a gale, and from directly behind me. If I kicked the ball high enough, the wind would do the rest.

And if I kicked a goal, Diggers Gully would win the Grand Final!

Both teams crowded down into the goal square. The Red Hills players would try to stop the ball or touch it, my team would try to shepherd it through the goals. Only Ryan and I remained in the centre. And the umpire.

'Don't take too long,' he said,

eyeing the huge black clouds that
swirled and boiled just overhead.

Ryan stood on the mark, his face
screwed up against the stinging rain.
'In your dreams, Kung-fu!'

I reckoned he was probably right.
But Boots Cooper thought I could kick

it, and he was the best footballer in the world.

Suddenly I realised that Boots Cooper *wanted* me to break his record!

I would do it for him. And not just for him, but for my whole team.

Lining up the goals, I began trotting forwards to take my kick.

16
Hip-and-shoulder

I had taken about three steps when a strange, tingly sensation zizzed up and down my spine. My skin went all goose-bumpy. Weirdest of all, the hair on my head felt as if it was standing on end!

A spooky crackling noise started up in my ears.

Above me, right at the top of my vision, a bluish–white glow flickered once, twice, three times inside a pitch-black cloud.

And something weird was going on
next to Ryan's foot. A patch of ground
about the size of a hand was glowing
with the same bluish–white light as
the cloud.

The crackling noise became louder.
Ryan must have heard it too,

because a puzzled expression crossed his face.

His hair was sticking straight up!

Suddenly I realised what was going on.

'Look out!' I yelled.

Dropping the ball, I rushed forward

and launched myself straight at Ryan. He was too surprised to duck. Crunch! Everyone watching said it was the best hip-and-shoulder they ever saw! Both of us flew about three metres, then rolled along the wet, slippery ground.

Behind us there was a blinding flash. A huge explosion ripped through the air. The ground heaved underneath us.

'What happened?' groaned Ryan, looking around with a dazed expression.

I spat out a mouthful of dirt and grass. 'We nearly got fried.'

17
Champion

I had read about it once in a book about surviving natural disasters. It said that if lightning is about to strike near you, you sometimes feel a tingly sensation and hear a crackling noise.

The book didn't say anything about a bluish–white glow. I guess that was caused by the gold nugget. Gold is one of the best conductors. The bolt of lightning went for it like iron to a magnet.

If I hadn't skittled Ryan, he would have been fried to a crisp!

There was nothing left of the nugget, just a big black hole in the ground.

Afterwards, when the storm had passed by and it was safe to go back onto the oval, they let me have my kick. But the wind had died down and I didn't even go close to making the distance.

So we lost the Grand Final and I lost my gold nugget.

But when I went to bed that night I didn't feel as if I had lost anything. I had saved someone's life; I had equalled Kenny Boots Cooper's eleven-year-old goal-kicking record; and, after the game, the best Aussie Rules footballer had shaken my hand and said that if I kept playing the way

I did in the Grand Final, one day
I would be an AFL champion!

And the way I figured it, that was
worth more than all the gold in the
world.

From Justin D'Ath

Bendigo, where I live, used to be a gold-mining town. All through the bush behind my house there are old mine shafts and mullock heaps. Whenever it's been raining, I go up there looking for gold. One day I hope to find a nugget like the one Austin found.

From Rachel Tonkin

I've never played football, but my son Patrick played great football. He was training to be a footy star until he discovered he was too short for the regional team. Our dog, who hated chasing footballs, was very pleased when Patrick took up running instead.